CH00858907

Baines

Text copyright © Frances Usher 1994
Illustrations copyright © Kate Aldous 1994

First published in Great Britain in 1994
by Simon & Schuster Young Books
Campus 400
Maylands Avenue
Hemel Hempstead
Herts HP2 7EZ

Typeset in 16/24pt Bembo by Goodfellow & Egan Ltd, Cambridge,
England
Printed and bound in Portugal by Ediçoes ASA

British Library Cataloguing in Publication Data available

ISBN 0 7500 1490 3
ISBN 0 7500 1491 1 (pb)

Frances Usher

Beach Baby

Illustrated by Kate Aldous

SIMON & SCHUSTER
YOUNG BOOKS

Chapter One

Belinda was a Beach Baby. She was a
Beach Baby right from the start.

When she was tiny, her mum used to
wrap her up warm and safe and carry
her out of the cottage. They'd go
through the gate and down the twenty-
seven steps that led to the beach.

Then Mum would carry her right to
the edge of the sea.

"Look, Belinda," she'd say.

She held Belinda up so she could see
the waves turning and turning.

"You're my Beach Baby," said Mum.

And Belinda would hold out her tiny
fingers to the sea and laugh and laugh.

When she was bigger, they made beautiful sand castles. And when she was bigger still, and went to the village school, Mum would meet her out and they'd have a picnic on the beach.

Belinda's cousins Ross and David came too. She'd run and run with the boys all the way to the sea.

Sometimes, at night, storms came roaring up. The waves smashed on the rocks below the cottage.

But in the morning the sun would shine again and Belinda would run across the clean sands and think she lived in the best place in the whole world.

Oh, Belinda was a Beach Baby all right.

But then, suddenly, something horrible happened.

"Belinda," Mum said one day. "There's something I have to tell you."

"What?" asked Belinda.

"We're going away," said Mum. "Going away for good."

Chapter Two

"Going away?" said Belinda. "Where? Why?"

"Well," said Mum. "I've made up my mind. I'm going to be a teacher."

"You can be a teacher," said Belinda. "Why not be a teacher at our school?"

"No," said Mum. "I have to go to college to study. And the college is a long way away."

"I don't want to go a long way away," said Belinda. She felt funny inside. "I want to stay here."

Mum gave her a hug.

"It will be all right," she said. "We're going to live in a big town. It will be fun. Look at these pictures."

Belinda didn't want to look.

"This is the college where I'm going to study," said Mum. "Isn't it nice?"

"No," said Belinda.

"And this is our new flat," said Mum.

"It's horrible," said Belinda.

Mum sighed.

"I'm sorry," she said. "But we have to go. You'll get used to the idea."

But Belinda didn't get used to the idea.

"You're lucky," said her cousin Ross. "Going to live in a town."

Belinda shook her head. "I like this cottage," she said. "I like the beach."

"I wish we were going," said her cousin David.

Belinda ran up to her bedroom.

She stood by the window, looking down at the beach. The seagulls were wheeling and turning in the sky, screaming at each other, looking for food.

"I'll hate living in the town," said Belinda. "I know I will. I'll never, never get used to it."

Chapter Three

All too soon, the day came for Mum
and Belinda to move.

First, she had to leave school.

"I've had a good idea, children," said
her teacher. "We must do something
really nice on Belinda's last day, because
we're going to miss her very much.
Let's have a lesson on the beach."

It was a beautiful sunny day. The tide
was out and there were pools among the
rocks.

The teacher showed them limpets, clinging so tightly to the rocks they couldn't be moved. Someone found a crab and someone else saw a starfish on the sand.

"My last day," Belinda kept thinking. "My last day."

At going home time, Belinda was given a big card with everyone's name in it.

"Don't forget us," said her friends. "Come back and see us."

"I promise," said Belinda.

Everything was packed up at the cottage, ready for the morning, so Mum and Belinda went out for supper.

They went to the pub by the beach. It was called The Captain's Cabin. Ross and David, Auntie and Uncle, Mum and Belinda sat outside in the warm dusk, eating their supper.

"Cheer up, Belinda," said Uncle. "You'll like it when you get there."

"Yes," said Belinda, trying to smile.

She jumped down on the sands with Ross and David. They all ran towards the misty sea.

Then Belinda turned and looked back. She saw the grown-ups at the table, saw the cottage on the cliffs.

"I don't want to go," she whispered. "I don't."

"Hush," said the waves. "Hush . . . hush . . . hush . . ."

Chapter Four

After that, there was no time for
Belinda to feel sad. She was much too
busy moving to the town. There was
such a lot to do.

"Hurry, Belinda," Mum kept saying.
"Help me do this . . . Quickly . . .
Quickly . . . Quickly."

Belinda felt as if she'd never stop
being out of breath.

Everything was completely different in the town.

When she woke up in the mornings now, she didn't hear the waves on the beach. She heard traffic roaring past.

When she looked out of her bedroom window, she didn't see rocks and the sea. She saw grass and blocks of flats.

When she and Mum went out, they didn't go running down to the sands. They had to cross busy streets.

Zoom . . . Zoom . . . Zoom . . . went the cars.

"Careful, Belinda," said Mum every day. "Look both ways."

On wet days, they were splashed with spray. Swish . . . Swish . . . Swish.

But it wasn't sea spray.

21

"Help, you'll be late for school,"
Mum said. "We must hurry, Belinda.
I've got a big day at college today."

Mum always kissed her goodbye at
the school gates.

"See you this afternoon, love," she'd
say. "Must rush. Bye."

The school seemed very big at first. It wasn't like the village school.

The teacher was kind. The children showed Belinda what to do. But Belinda felt lost for a long time.

She kept thinking about her friends in the village school. She wanted to be back there. She wanted to live in the cottage again.

But then she made a friend.

Chapter Five

Her name was Zoe. She was in the same class as Belinda. She sat at the same table.

One day, when they were all drawing a big picture together, she lent Belinda her blue crayon.

"Colour the sea with that," she said.

Belinda said, "The sea isn't that colour."

"Isn't it?" said Zoe. "I thought it was."

"It's all sorts of colours," said
Belinda. "Green and brown and purple
and grey. And sometimes blue as well.
You have to put lots of colours in it."

"I've never seen the sea," said Zoe.
"Only on the telly."

Belinda stared at her.

What would it be like, never to have
seen the sea? She couldn't think.

She began telling Zoe all about the
cottage where she used to live, about the
beach. They talked all afternoon as they
worked on the picture.

Just talking about her old home made
Belinda happy.

After that, Zoe and Belinda were
friends. They sat together in school.
They played together in the
playground.

Soon, Belinda started going to tea at
Zoe's flat, and Zoe started coming to
Belinda's flat.

On Saturdays, Belinda's mum or
Zoe's mum took them to the swimming
pool or gym class. It was fun.

Slowly, slowly, Belinda got used to living in the town.

She knew her way round school. She could cross streets. She knew the bus stops, and the supermarkets.

But, somewhere, inside her mind, she was still a Beach Baby.

Inside her mind, she still ran on the sands towards the sea. Somewhere, inside her mind, the waves were still turning and turning.

Chapter Six

It was spring. A cat was washing itself
in a sunny corner below Belinda's flat.
Mum was doing her college homework.

"Mum," said Belinda.

Mum looked up.

"It must be nice on the beach today,"
said Belinda. "You know, on our old
beach."

Mum rubbed her head. Then she
smiled.

"Yes," she said.

That was all. But a week or two later,
Mum began to talk about a holiday. A
holiday by the sea.

"We can't go back to our cottage, of course," she said. "New people live there now. But we could stay with Uncle and Auntie for a few days."

"And Ross and David?" asked Belinda.

Mum nodded.

"Can we go to the beach?" asked Belinda. "Can we spend every day on the beach?"

Mum nodded again, smiling.

Belinda felt a rush of joy inside. She gave Mum a big hug.

Then she said, "Can Zoe come too?"

It took time to fix everything. But at last it was settled. Zoe would go with them on holiday.

The night before they went, Belinda was too excited to sleep.

Every time she closed her eyes, she thought she was on the beach, and white seagulls were swooping over the waves.

Chapter Seven

"Are we nearly there?" Zoe kept saying. "Shall we see the sea in a minute?"

She knelt up on the coach seat to look out of the window.

"Soon," said Mum. "Have another sandwich, girls. It will help the time to pass."

The coach drove on and on.

After a time, Belinda and Zoe felt sleepy. Before they knew it, their eyes closed.

Then Mum was waking them up.
"Look out of the window, girls," she
said.

They looked. They were driving
down a long hill.

"Oh!" said Belinda.

"The sea!" cried Zoe.

Down below them lay the village.
And, beyond that, lay the sea.

In a minute, they were driving
through the village.

"There's the church," said Belinda.
"And that's my old school . . ."

The children were in the playground.
Belinda waved and waved.

Then the coach turned a corner and
they were there.

They stood up and went to the door.
Auntie was there to meet them. The
driver took their bags out of the coach
for them.

"It's lovely to be back," said Mum.
"Isn't it, Belinda?"

But Belinda wasn't listening.

She was standing on her own,
breathing big breaths of sea air.

After Auntie had given them tea, and shown Belinda and Zoe the little room where they were going to sleep, they all walked over the cliffs to the sea.

Belinda looked at their old cottage. All the curtains were different. It felt strange to think of someone else living there.

But the steps to the beach were the same.

"One . . . two . . . three . . . four . . ."
the girls started to count.

". . . five . . . six . . . seven . . ."
everyone joined in.

"Oh, I'm out of breath," said Mum.
But Belinda and Zoe went on counting.

". . . twenty-three . . . twenty-four . . ."
Belinda could hear the waves.

". . . twenty-five . . . twenty-six . . .
twenty-SEVEN."

They were on the beach.

Chapter Eight

When she thought about that holiday afterwards, Belinda could never make up her mind which part was best.

One day Uncle took them out in his boat. He took Belinda and Zoe, Ross and David, right round the bay.

The boat bobbed over the waves.

"I might be sick," said Zoe. But she wasn't.

Another day, they had a big picnic on the beach.

Lots of Belinda's old friends came. They played games and lay in the sun. The gulls were wheeling overhead, crying and calling.

Belinda pushed her feet into the sand and covered them right up. She felt absolutely happy.

Every day, she and Zoe ran and ran
on the beach. They splashed in the
waves and watched the tiny fish in the
rock pools.

"I never thought the sea would be like
this," said Zoe. "It's even better than the
park at home."

"Much, much better," said Belinda.

She wished the holiday would go on
for ever. But it didn't.

One morning, when she woke up,
she lay and thought of all the nice things
she and Zoe would do that day.

Then she remembered.

They were leaving on the coach after
breakfast.

"No," she said. "No."

She looked at Zoe. Zoe was still
asleep.

Very quietly, she got up and dressed.
She opened the bedroom door and
listened. Everything was quiet.

Then she tiptoed down the stairs and
let herself out of the house.

Chapter Nine

It was still very early.

The tide was out. Sand stretched away on every side, clean and washed and empty.

As Belinda walked across the beach, she left a thin line of footprints.

"Don't be scared," she told herself. "This is your home. Your real home."

She climbed over the rocks until she found a dry, safe place to curl up.

A long time went by. Belinda stared
at their cottage on the cliffs and at the
gulls flying round and round it.

After a long, long time, she saw Mum
coming along the beach towards her.

She kept still.

"Belinda," Mum called. "Where are
you, Belinda?"

Belinda put her head up. Mum was
looking all round. "Where are you?" she
called again.

Belinda could see how worried she looked. She stood up.

"I'm here," she said.

Mum came running.

She took Belinda by the shoulders and shook her.

"How could you run off down here on your own?" she said. "I was so frightened."

"I couldn't help it," said Belinda. Then she started to cry.

"Oh, Belinda," said Mum.

She put her arms round her and held her tight.

"I don't want to go back," said Belinda. "I want to stay here."

"I know, love," said Mum. "But we have to go back. Think of poor Zoe. She'll want to go home to her mum, won't she?"

Belinda sniffed and nodded.

They started to walk along the beach, holding hands.

"I used to carry you along here," said Mum. "You were my Beach Baby."

"I remember," said Belinda.

Mum smiled. "Do you?" she said. "You were very small then."

"I do remember," said Belinda.

They went on walking.

"If you're a Beach Baby," said Mum, "you take it with you wherever you go. It'll be inside you for the rest of your life."

"Even in the town?" asked Belinda. "Even in the flat?"

"Oh, yes," said Mum. "Once a Beach Baby, always a Beach Baby."

Belinda began to feel a bit better.

She picked up a shell and put it in her pocket.

"One day," she said, "I'll live here again. When I'm older."

"Why not?" said Mum. "One day you might bring your own baby along here and show them the sea, like I showed you. Your own Beach Baby."

"Yes, I might," said Belinda.

And she and Mum went on walking along the sands.

Look out for other books in the *yellow* Storybooks series:

Alice Alone by Shirley Isherwood

Alice and her little brother Scooter love staying on their grandfather's farm. But one night Grandfather is very late coming home – is anything wrong?

A Magic Birthday by Adèle Geras

Maddy can't wait until her birthday party. All her special friends are coming and there is going to be a conjuring show. But Maddy is worried that there will be one important thing missing . . .

The Laughing Snowman by Anne Forsyth

During the snow, Emma is woken up in the middle of the night by the sound of laughter. And when she peeks outside, she sees the most astonishing sight!

Khumalo's Blanket by Iain Macdonald

Khumalo's village is in danger, and he must choose between his most treasured possession and the good of all his people.

I Want That Pony! by Christine Pullein-Thompson

Sophy loves Flash, the pony that lives down the lane. But the pony belongs to somebody else, who doesn't want to let Sophy have anything to do with her beloved pony . . .

Storybooks can be ordered from your local bookshop, or they can be ordered straight from the publisher. For more information, write to: *The Sales Department, Simon & Schuster Young Books, Campus 400, Maylands Avenue, Hemel Hempstead HP2 7EZ.*